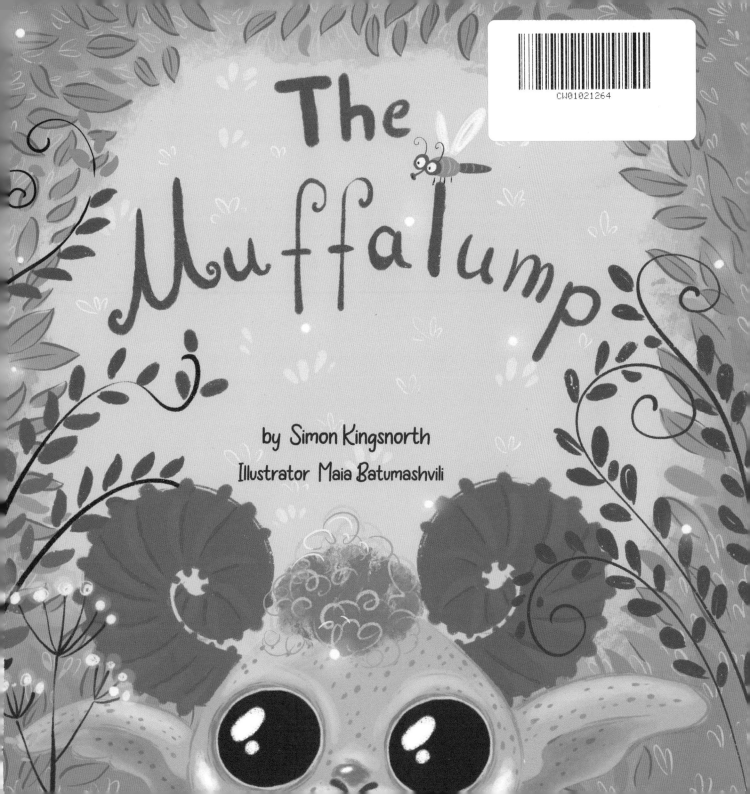

The Muffalump

by Simon Kingsnorth

Illustrator Maia Batumashvili

CW01021264

They hide in the woods,

they hide in the dark

They hide in the trees,

they chew on the bark

Their eyes are like diamonds,

their tails like pigs

Their horns are all shiny,

they snort and they dig

They look quite like sheep

but crossed with flamingos

They're quite fond of funny jokes,

cartoons and bingo

They're really quite ticklish,

especially their tummies

They can't get enough

of their Daddies and Mummies

They can't drive a car

and they can't fly a plane

But they do love

to travel on really fast trains

They're lovely and sweet

but they find us quite loud

They climb up to hide

when we come around

They don't eat the leaves

and they don't eat the trees

To eat up their dinner

they need quite strong knees

If you watch the woods

you might see one leap

as they jump to the sky

for a fluffy sweet treat

They bite the marshmallow

that makes up the clouds

They chew it all up

and then float way back down

So look for the eyes

poking out of the trees

And look to the skies

for the jumping pink knees

If you see a cloud with

some teeth mark shaped bumps

You might just have seen

a pink Muffalump

Do those clouds have teeth mark shaped bumps?
Could there be, could there be
a pink Muffalump?

Muffalumps are shy and mysterious creatures.
They are difficult to find as they hide in the trees.

But watch the skies carefully for their unique features
And you might just spot some jumping pink knees.

For Oz and Dexter   © Simon Kingsnorth